To Jason and Tina – forever friends
C.F.

For Chris
for keeping me smiling
and for the many many cups of tea
with all my love
G.R.

First published in Great Britain in 2011 by
Gullane Children's Books
185 Fleet Street, London, EC4A 2HS
www.gullanebooks.com

1 3 5 7 9 10 8 6 4 2

Text © Claire Freedman 2011
Illustrations © Gemma Raynor 2011

The right of Claire Freedman and Gemma Raynor to be identified as the author and illustrator of this work
has been asserted by them in accordance with the Copyright, Designs and Patents Act, 1988.
A CIP record for this title is available from the British Library.

ISBN: 978-1-86233-801-2

Printed and bound in China

Mimi Make-Believe

Northumberland County Council	
3 0132 02077610 5	
Askews & Holts	Sep-2011
JF	£10.99

Claire Freedman

illustrated by
Gemma Raynor

GULLANE
CHILDREN'S BOOKS

Mimi loved to play make-believe.
She pretended she was a fearless explorer,
trekking through the thick jungle.

Sometimes she was a
Knight in Shining Armour.
Bravely she chased off big puffing
dragons, to rescue the princess
trapped in the castle!

Or she was Mimi the Mighty Raccoon,
saving raccoons and beavers in trouble!

But, secretly, Mimi was rather lonely.
She dreamt of having a real friend.
Someone to share her adventures!

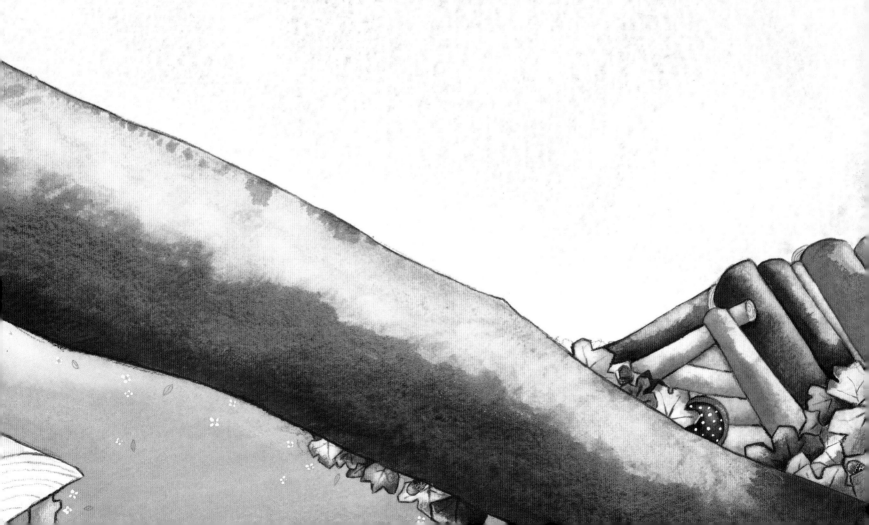

One day there was a lot of hustle and bustle down the lane. Bursting with curiosity and excitement, Mimi took a peep.

"Oh!" she cried. "Someone new is moving in!"
Mimi watched as Beaver unloaded all
his belongings. She couldn't help
daydreaming a little . . .

"Just imagine!" she thought.
"If Beaver and I became best friends,
we could play lots of games together!
Like Cowboys and Sheriffs.
We'd ride our wild horses,
and lasso wicked bandits and . . . !"

Mimi was so excited, she walked right
up to Beaver's house to say "hello".
But suddenly she felt shy.
"Beaver won't want to play silly
games with me!" she said.
"He'll be too busy unpacking!"

So Mimi turned tail
and scurried home,
before Beaver spotted her.

The next morning, Mimi
was playing astronauts.
"If Beaver and I became friends,"
she smiled to herself, "we could
build ourselves the biggest space
rocket in the whole universe.
We'd fly to the moon, meet
funny aliens and . . . !"

Mimi rushed round to Beaver's house.
But suddenly she stopped in her tracks.
"Beaver won't be interested in playing with me,"
she sighed shyly. "He'll have his own friends."

Hurriedly, Mimi pitter-pattered
back home, all alone again.

The following day, Mimi was playing Desert Islands.
She was making a huge flag, to wave at
any passing rescue ships, when suddenly . . .

kER-SPLOSH!

She heard a very loud splash close by! Then . . .

"**Help!**" came a loud cry.
"**The sharks are after me! HELP!**"
Mimi rushed to look...

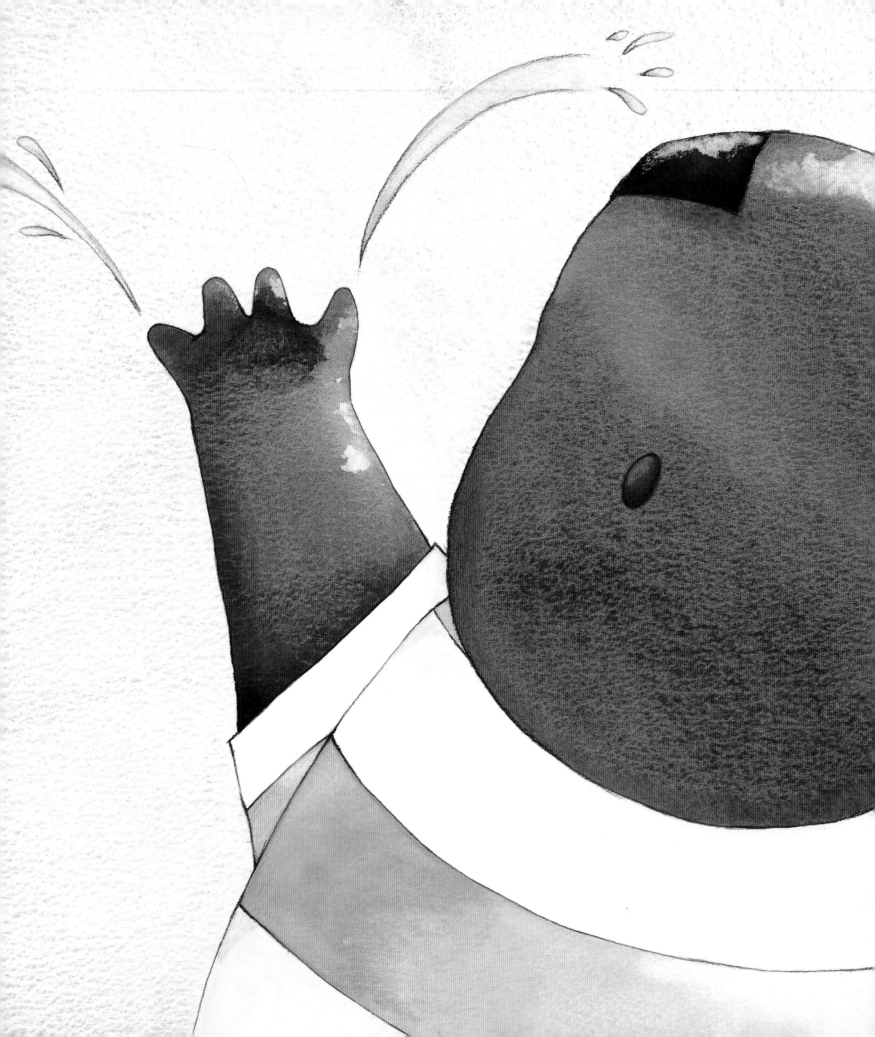

Beaver was in the water!

"Never fear, Mimi the Mighty Raccoon is here!"
she shouted.
"I'll rescue you!"

Bravely Mimi leapt into the water and pulled Beaver safely out.
"You're safe from the sharks now!" she panted.

Then she had a thought.
What sharks...?!

"Whoops!" giggled Beaver. "They were **pretend sharks!**
I'm having an adventure!"

"An adventure?" gasped Mimi. "What kind of adventure?"

"I'm playing pirates!" Beaver laughed.
"Look, there's my. . .

"SHIP!"

Floating nearby was a magnificent pirate ship.
"Of course, you need two bold, fearless pirates
to crew a proper pirate ship. . ." said Beaver.
"Treasure Island here we come!" shouted Mimi.

And the two pirates set sail on the high seas,
happily dreaming up their next big and exciting adventure –
together!